The Missing Bezel

J. Lee Porter, Ed Teja

Nomadic Giant

Nomadic Giant, LLC.

Contents

Prologue

E loy leaned back against a smooth rock and watched the lazy motion of the Magdapio River as it flowed by.

It was cooler here than in the pretend village the movie had built further up the bank. And here he could sit and eat a pineapple, cutting off chunks with the knife his father had given him.

The movie set held little interest for him. The presence of an occasional American actor meant even less.

The crew were all right and sometimes gave him odd jobs to do. A chance for a twelve-year-old to earn money was rare, and he liked helping out his parents.

They worked on the set too. His mother spent her days in the cooking tent, providing meals for the crew. His father did carpentry, building whatever the movie company needed.

Right now, the movie people were paying them good money, but his father had warned him it wouldn't go on long. Eventually they would leave, go to Manila and then back to the US. When that happened, life in Pagsanjan would return to normal and that meant much less work.

Today, there was little to do. Someone said that the crew were staging a scene, whatever that meant.

A fat American, new to the set, came storming out of a hut. He heard it was the office of the production. The man's face was dark, and he came to the river, straight to where Eloy sat.

"That asshole," the man said. "What stupidity!"

Eloy cut off a large piece of pineapple and held it up to the man. "Sweet pineapple makes sour things better," he said.

The man glared for a second. Eloy realized he hadn't seen him and had been talking to himself. Then he smiled and took the pineapple and popped it into his mouth.

"Thank you," he said. "That was sweet."

"If you are still angry, you can have more," Eloy said.

The man chuckled. "That's nice of you, but I'll keep getting angry again, I'm afraid." He held up an arm, rotating it. "It's because of this watch."

Eloy squinted. The watch was big and beautiful. "How can something so lovely make you angry?" he asked.

The man put his hands on his hips and stared out at the river. "You like it?"

"What I can see," Eloy said.

The man slipped it off and handed it to him. "The damn director said I can't wear it for the shoot, that it will be too distracting. Hell, if that's the case, then I'm not doing a very good job acting, am I? If I do my job, no one will notice the watch."

Eloy's heart pounded. The watch was heavy and the most beautiful thing he'd ever seen. He loved mechanical things, learning how they worked, and trying to make them work better. He'd fixed every bicycle in the village of Pagsanjan at one time or another.

But he'd never seen anything like this. Its steady ticking made it feel alive in his hand.

"What do you think?" the man asked him. "Shouldn't a good actor be able to wear almost anything and convince the audience?"

"I know nothing of acting," Eloy said, transfixed by the timepiece. The bezel that encircled the crystal had hours marked on it and it moved. "But if you want to wear it... what if this beautiful watch did not look so fancy?" he asked.

The man looked at him. "What do you mean?"

He twisted the bezel. "This part is very colorful. If it were not there, maybe no one would notice the watch so much."

The man smiled and held out his hand. Reluctantly, Eloy handed it back.

The man looked closely at the watch. "I hadn't thought of that," he said, turning the bezel. "But you are right, and I'll bet it comes off easily." He smiled. "Can I borrow your knife?"

Eloy handed the knife to him, handle first, as his father had taught him. The man sat on a rock and used the point to poke at the watch.

"Looks like it's just fitted in," he said.

That made good sense, Eloy thought, watching the man dig the point in.

He heard a snap. "There," the man said.

Eloy looked and saw that the colorful bezel was gone. The man had popped it off. But where had it gone? As he looked around for the piece, the man handed Eloy the knife back and stood up.

"Now, let's see what he says. It looks plain enough.

Eloy watched him go, then started hunting around the area. That pretty, circular piece had to go somewhere.

On his hands and knees, he looked carefully through the weeds and grass until he found it, stuck between two rocks, right at the edge of the river.

It had gone further than he would have guessed.

As he stood, he saw the actor coming back again. Quickly, he stuffed it in his pants pocket. If the man saw he had it, he might want it back.

But he didn't.

The man held out a US five-dollar bill.

"Brilliant thinking," he told the boy. "Even Frank couldn't find a good excuse for making me take it off now."

Then, puffed up, proud of winning his point, the fat man walked away.

"Where did you get five dollars?" his mother asked him later.

"From a fat American working on the movie. He had a problem with his watch and I helped him fix it." Then he caught himself. "He fixed it, but I came up the idea of what to do."

She pursed her lips. "You are good with mechanical things."

"I like them. You can figure them out if you are careful."

"And you like watches?"

He nodded. "The ones I have seen are very interesting." He decided not to mention that he had taken his father's watch apart once. No one knew.

She smiled. "Your cousin in Manila is a watch repairman. He has his own shop and his mother told me he wants an apprentice. None of their children know anything about watches and they don't care much about learning."

"Why not?"

She looked at her boy. "Tell me, Eloy, do you think you would like to go to Manila and live with your aunt and uncle and learn about watches?"

Eloy couldn't hide his excitement. "More than anything."

She nodded. "Your father and I will talk about it. When this movie is done, I am going to Manila to see my sister. If you go with me, we can talk to your cousin. It is a good job."

Eloy went to bed that night as optimistic about his future as he could ever remember being. A watchmaker worked in a shop, out of the streets. He had a trade. He was paid to work with intricate and wondrous machinery.

What could be better?

The Missing Bezel

L ex Craig took a deep breath and looked at the email on his laptop.

He didn't like checking his email so early in the morning. That was always a mistake, but business was slow.

He'd been hoping for a follow-up inquiry from a buyer who had seemed interested in a pricey set of Kris knives he'd recently put on his website.

Instead, he found a message from a law firm, asking him to call.

A message from lawyers was seldom good, but this message included some of his favorite words: "We would like to discuss a commission for locating a specific item."

He sent the email to the printer in his office and then, still in his robe and carrying his second cup of morning coffee, Lex Craig went down the hallway and entered the small bedroom that was his home office.

He glanced at the page on the printer. It could wait. Setting the coffee on his desk, he opened the curtains to let in the wonderful morning sunshine. This was the kind of day that had made him fall in love with his small house on the California coastline.

Even sitting at his desk, he could look out over the ocean and standing at the bay windows staring out to sea made him feel like a millionaire.

He wouldn't be able to enjoy that for much longer unless business picked up.

The house was paid for, but his property taxes and the cost of living here... the cost of everything had gone through the roof at the same time that his business had begun falling off.

It had been a good run, and he loved his work.

"Lex Craig, Global Picker," his card proudly said. "Buying and selling the odd and unusual."

Traveling the world had been his dream. He'd gotten a job with a coffee importer and started doing just that. Later, having learned the ropes, he went off on his own, buying things he thought he could sell for a profit.

He'd done well, hunting down silver snuff boxes, Kris knives in the night markets of Kuala Lumpur and Indonesia, and various rare items found in estate sales in Europe and Australia.

He had found this house and bought it for cash, right after he found that matching set of hand-carved teak chests and sold them to a private collector in Monaco.

But the world got more sophisticated, and people learned they could sell their own stuff online. It had gotten easy to do through eBay and all the other sites.

That meant it was harder to find inventory, especially high end. And hunting was more expensive, too.

Along with his living costs, the costs of travel to track down new inventory had skyrocketed. He was going to need a new business model as well as move to a cheaper base.

But business, he knew, didn't get better... you had to do something to make that happen. He went to the printer and picked up the email, standing there, reading it over several times as he sipped his coffee.

He knew it by heart by then, but it told him nothing certain.

"Discussing a commission," in his experience, did not always mean paying one.

But, if it did, he needed to fund another trip to Asia, to restock. There were still some things available in the few remaining night markets that he could always find a buyer for.

He went to the window and looked out across the ocean, seeing the way the sun rising behind his house reflected on it. He'd bought the house at a good time.

In the current economy he would never be able to afford it. No Way.

He was considering selling it. He'd get enough to buy himself something nice in a more affordable place, like Mexico or maybe Panama. He needed to visit Boquete soon again anyway, and he might take extra time to do a little house hunting.

First, however, he needed to talk to the lawyer. The number had an east coast area code, so, he took his phone from its charger and called. The receptionist cheerfully, efficiently, put him through to a Mr. Bland.

"Ah, Mr. Craig," he said, thanking him for calling. "We would like to begin by hiring you for a consultation with our client."

"Who is?"

"Anonymous, for the moment."

"Consulting about what?"

The man paused. "Watch parts. Old-fashioned mechanical watches. We understand you are something of an expert on such things."

"I'm an expert on finding them, evaluating them. I can't fix them."

"Exactly what is needed," Mr. Bland said. "Are you available for a consultation this week? The client is in a rush."

"Where?"

"New Jersey."

He groaned. The out-of-pocket costs would be a lot. "I'd have to fly..."

"We will provide a first-class round-trip ticket and pay you a thousand dollars for your time."

"A thousand for the consultation and another thousand for the two travel days. You will have to sign and return a nondisclosure agreement that says you won't ever tell anyone about this meeting."

This deal was starting to sound interesting. Even after catching up on his current bills, he'd have enough to make the trip to Panama.

"I can leave in the morning," he told Mr. Bland.

"Have you got a suit and tie?" Mr. Bland asked. "The client is a stickler for such things."

"I do." Somewhere.

"Excellent. I'll send you a ticket along with the nondisclosure," the man said. "It will be there within the hour. The messenger will wait for you to read and sign the agreement and then return with it."

"Fine."

Who used messengers anymore? He could sign it, scan it in and email it back.

"The client's people will pick you up in the baggage area."

The client's people?

This got more interesting all the time.

Being met at the airport by a liveried chauffeur was a new experience. So was being swept into a gated mansion at the top of a hill in a surprisingly wooded area of New Jersey.

The biggest surprise was learning that he was meeting the secretive Tucker Trichet. When the chauffeur told him, he wracked his brain for all he knew about the man. All he could come up with was that his father was an industrialist and when he died, Tucker took over and dumped heavy industry in favor of higher tech, more contemporary investments.

And had gotten filthy rich.

A butler met him at the door, and with an appropriate butler scowl, let him in. Just into the entry hall.

A personal assistant, named Clyde, nervously escorted him up a huge, curved flight of stairs that looked to be made of marble and edged with a mahogany handrail, into an office that looked like an English gentleman's club.

It reminded him of The Explorers Club in London, where Lex had once had a quick drink when he delivered a lovely crystal-handled dagger to a man who would later claim to have taken it from a savage in Borneo even though he knew it had been made in Jakarta.

In the study stood Tucker Trichet, a thin, stern-faced man of medium height. Lex found him surprisingly nondescript, except for piercing eyes.

Clyde told Trichet Lex's name and then obsequiously backed out of the room.

Tucker Trichet stared at Lex, appraising him. "You are the watch expert... the expert on locating watch parts, I mean."

Lex was glad the man had corrected himself. He didn't seem the kind who would take kindly to having servants, which meant almost everyone, correct him.

"As much as anyone is," he said.

"What do you know about Rolex watches from the seventies?"

"That the GMT is the most famous and a beautiful timepiece."

The man gave him a thin smile. "And what GMT watch of that period is the most famous of them all?"

Lex didn't miss a beat. "The 1675 that Marlon Brando wore in the movie Apocalypse Now."

A maid came in and Tucker nodded. As she went to a bar and fixed them each a tall drink, Lex felt like he'd passed some test.

"Do you know where that watch is now?"

Lex took the drink and raised the glass. "He gave it to his daughter when she graduated from Brown University. Later it was auctioned off for something like two million dollars."

"One point nine million, when you factored in the fees from the auction house," Tucker said. "Would you like to see it?"

Lex swallowed. "Hell, yes!" he said, forgetting himself.

Tucker nodded and led him into a room that looked like part of a museum. Collectibles and paintings hung on the walls (he thought he recognized some of the art), and more were in glass display cases (netsuke and tiny boxes), and, in the middle of the room was a pedestal with a glass box on it. Tucker led him there and when Lex looked, he saw it. A translucent stand held it so you could see the face, and by ducking down, see the back, where Marlon Brando had scratched his name in the case.

"M. Brando."

"My father bought it because of its association with Brando, whom he admired, and the movie, which he loathed. A piece of history on two levels, from his perspective. For my part, I can't abide having a stupid broken watch sitting around."

"Broken?"

"The bezel is missing."

Lex knew the story. "Brando took it off because the director thought the watch was distracting."

"And no one knows what happened to the fucking bezel!" Tucker said. Clearly, that upset him.

"You can buy a replacement bezel for about a hundred bucks," Lex said. He was trying to get a handle on what the man expected from him.

"A replacement bezel would be new. The originals faded over time. Their colors shifted. A new bezel would have bright colors and look fake."

"Buy an older watch and take the bezel off it. I do that all the time."

Tucker Trichet looked daggers at him. "That wouldn't be the original bezel."

He turned and stormed out of the room. Unsure what to do, Lex took a sip of his drink. "A tad OCD, are we?" he mumbled under his breath. Then he followed his host back to the study.

"So, do I have the right man?" Trichet asked as he motioned Lex to a plush leather chair.

"To do what, exactly?"

"To find the original bezel."

"I'm not sure where I'd start looking," he said.

Trichet laughed and pointed to a thick folder sitting on the coffee table. "I've researched the movie thoroughly. I'd hopped one of the crew had found the bezel, but no such luck. At least, it wasn't reported. But the movie was filmed in The Philippines and the bezel was definitely on the watch when he arrived, and it was gone when he left. That suggests a place to start looking."

Searching The Philippines would give him a chance to find a lot of other treasures to resell, so, even though he put the chance of finding the original bezel on a par with getting Vladimir Putin a Nobel Peace Prize, the effort wouldn't be wasted.

"That could take me a while," Lex said.

"It's likely in Luzon," he said. "Start there. Talk to locals who worked on the movie."

They worked on it fifty years ago. Fat chance most were still around.

"I'll pay your expenses and pay you a day rate. If you find it within six months, I'll give you a $20k bonus."

Lex felt he was beginning to understand the man now. "I'm guessing you picked that bonus because it's the current price of a new Rolex GMT, correct?"

Trichet nodded. "And therefore, seems appropriate. I do like things to be appropriate. And efficient. Can you leave today?"

He could.

"I'll expect daily reports," Trichet said. "I want details of your efforts and the results."

Of course he did.

Iba, on Luzon's west coast, northwest of Manila, wasn't a big place. And while a lot of people remembered a movie had been filmed there, what they remembered was an older uncle or aunt or parent who had been a kid running amok on the set.

Three days spent talking to the older people, especially people in the trades, going into watch repair places and small shops that made and repaired jewelry on the off chance someone had found and hawked the bezel, came up with nothing. Well, he acquired a few jade pieces and some other things, but didn't see a single watch bezel.

Stopping for a beer at a food stall, the old man who ran it gave him an odd look. "You looking for something? I've seen you running around asking questions of people."

Lex told him about the movie.

"I'm hoping I can find someone who was on the set at the time."

"I remember the craziness when that bunch came," the man said. "But not that much got filmed here."

"Why not?"

"Typhoon Olga. It hit just when they wanted to start," he said.

"You remember that?"

"My father helped build some things, but his brother was a fisherman. When the storm approached, we took his boats over to a shelter and waited out the storm. When we came back, we found the typhoon had wrecked almost everything the men had built."

"But I'm sure they filmed the movie on Luzon," Lex said.

The man nodded. "But they rebuilt the sets somewhere else."

"Where?"

He shrugged. "If you go by the market in the early morning, you can ask the old lady who sells fish. Her husband was a carpenter, so she might know."

Satisfied that he'd learn something useful, Lex went to his room and napped through the afternoon heat, then went out in the evening and located a few items that he could sell. He packaged them up and sent them home.

Happily, the next morning he found the woman. And she did remember the filming. "After the big storm wrecked the things my husband and the others built, the Americans went away for a time," she said. "Then they hired people to build them again in Pagsanjan." She waved a hand. "They wanted us to go, but that is far, way the other side of Manila."

After he arranged transportation, Lex sent Trichet a report. A detailed report. He even included photos of the old woman and the food stall owner.

Trichet's reply was rapid — an enthusiastic phone call urging Lex to "get your ass there!"

He sounded happy, as if he was finally getting his money's worth.

According to the guidebook Lex had brought along, Pagsanjan was located in the delta formed by the confluence of the Balanac and Bumbungan rivers. Situated on a lagoon, it was far more sheltered from the possibility of further typhoons.

Probably to appease the insurance company.

Pagsanjan turned out to be a nice, smallish city, and he took a room at a pleasant hotel in the center of town, walking distance to the markets and people who might remember something about a now-nearly ancient movie.

Fifty years was a long time, and the world had changed a great deal.

After several days of eating meals at food stalls where he could talk to people and showing around pictures of a GMT 1675 bezel, he came across a woman who laughed when she saw the picture.

"My brother Eloy had one of those," she said. "I hadn't thought of it in years."

"You've seen it?"

"He showed it to me when I visited him in Manila. Eloy was so proud of it. I couldn't understand what was important about such a silly circle. He told me that, before I was born, a man let him hold the watch that it came from in his hands. Immediately, he loved it and knew what he wanted to do with his life. Our mother took him to Manila so he could work for our uncle. He was a great watch repair-man."

"Did he say where he got it?"

She shook her head sadly. "I don't recall. It was a long time ago. He was older than me and I only saw him when we visited Manila. If he told me, it wasn't important to me."

Lex's pulse raced. This sounded right. He couldn't believe he'd actually picked up the trail of the original, but she had no reason to lie. "Does he still have it?"

She laughed again. "He is dead now, and that was so long ago..."

His heart sank. "Dead?"

"A few years ago." She saw the look on his face and gave him a sympathetic smile. "You could talk to his son. He inherited the shop."

"The shop?"

"Uncle left the watch repair shop to my brother. Of course, it would be hard to earn a living repairing those kinds of watches these days and I'm sure my nephew has changed the business. But if Eloy kept that circle, his son, Manny, might know where it is."

Lex gave her a reward for her help, and with the address of the shop in his phone, he checked out of the hotel and headed for Manila.

He decided not to report this to Trichet. There was no value in getting his hopes up if this turned out to be a dead end. He was sure he was on the scent, but there was no telling what had happened to the bezel in Manila. It might have wound up as a replacement on someone's watch years ago.

He found Manny Aruda to be a cheerful young man with almost no knowledge of mechanical watches. Lex glanced around the shop and saw an array of cell phones and digital watches.

"Do you have parts for Rolex watches?" he asked.

The young man shook his head. "Nothing old fashioned," he said. "But I can get you a good price on a Fitbit. Even on Amazon, they cost over a hundred. I can get you a new one, in the box, for eighty-five. You check the price and see. Best price in Manila, maybe the world."

Lex showed him the picture of the bezel. "How about something like this? Have you seen one?"

The man squinted and shook his head. "My father had stuff like that... boxes and boxes of them. But no one has needed them in years."

"Do you still have them? Those boxes?"

Manny shrugged. "My wife cleaned out the shop after my father died, helped me upgrade it. But she maybe stored some."

"I'd be willing to pay for the chance to go through those," he said.

"No shit?" Manny looked excited.

"I'd give you a hundred to let me look, and another hundred if I find the one I'm looking for."

Manny grabbed his phone. "I'll call my wife."

Manny's wife, a sharp-eyed, thin woman named Rowena, had a storage unit that Manny neither knew nor cared about.

"Manny doesn't understand that these things can have value," she said. "I sold some of the watches his father had around on eBay."

"And the odd parts?" he asked and feeling the tension of being so close.

She shook her head. "I haven't had time to deal with them all." She pointed to shelves of boxes and jars, overflowing with bits and pieces. "For a hundred dollars, you can look."

"It will take me some time," he said.

"Take your time," she said. "But anything you find that you think you want... we will discuss the price."

"Of course," he said.

And so he started. There was no rhyme or reason that Lex could see in the way the parts were stored. A box might have watch springs, part of a movement, and an assortment of tiny screws.

There were a number of crystals and tension rings for bezels, and even bracelets for a couple of expensive Rolex watches. He put those things aside.

And he kept looking.

But there were no bezels.

One morning, Rowena came in to check on him. "Find anything you like yet?"

He pointed to the small stack of things he'd put aside. "A few things. But not the most important."

"So, you are hoping to find a particular piece?"

It dawned on him that he hadn't asked her about the bezel, just the parts that Eloy had stashed. He got the picture out of his pocket and showed it to her. "That."

She cocked her head and held up her hand, her finger and thumb making a circle. "It goes around the face of the watch?"

"Yes."

"Manny's father had a few of those."

"A few?"

"Different colors."

"But one exactly like that?"

"He was proud of it. Crazy story the old man told. He said he met a fat American when his parents worked on a movie set. The man took that piece off his watch for some reason. Manny's father thought it was beautiful. He picked it up and kept it."

Lex saw the look on her face. "And you still have it?"

She chuckled, a crafty look on her face. It was too bad Manny wasn't the one he had to deal with.

"The piece is more faded than your picture."

"I knew it would be."

She rubbed her hands together. "Manny's father he told me that little ring would be worth money one day. It seems he was right. It is worth a great deal of time and trouble to you."

"If it is the right one."

"Tomorrow," she said. "You keep looking here and find more things that please you. Tomorrow morning, I will bring it."

The next morning, she played her hand like a professional gambler. "Show me all the things you want," she said.

He pointed to a bowl of parts sitting on a table. She handed him a wooden box, like the kind that small broaches come in. As he opened the box, she looked through the things in the bowl.

His hands were sweaty as he stared at a classic, red and blue, "Pepsi" bezel insert for the GMT-Master. It hadn't faded as much as others of its age, but then it had been stored. Still the bright was now a vivid magenta and the royal blue looked like the blue of a summer sky.

It matched the story of the watch perfectly.

Lex knew there was no way in hell to know for certain what watch a particular bezel came from. Even experts couldn't tell. But all indications were that this was it.

Saying it was for sure would make him feel like he was scamming his client. But the man didn't give a damn about history. He wanted a complete watch. This bezel would give him closure.

Rowena looked up from the items that Lex had put in the bowl.

"Is that what you wanted?"

"It might be," he said.

"Some movie star wants his watch repaired after all these years?"

He nodded. "Something like that. The current owner."

She named a price. It was high. "Five thousand," she said. "For that bezel."

The woman was shrewd. She expected to haggle. That was good business.

"One thousand," he said.

"Four thousand," she said. "But you give me one hundred for the junk and tell Manny that's what you paid me. He has no head for business."

He imagined Tucker Trichet's voice on the phone when he called him with the news and smiled. Three thousand plus the hundred."

"Three thousand five hundred," she said. "Plus the hundred all in cash. And you pay today."

Lex knew this was her final offer.

"We need to go to the bank so I can cash travelers' checks."

She smiled. "I like banks."

She watched him put the bezel in his pocket and the other parts in a padded bag, then she locked the storage unit. Noticing, for the first time, that she had several similar keys on her ring, a thought occurred to him.

"I'll bet you have other storage units," he said.

She smiled. "Why would I have more?"

"A resourceful woman like you might have other family members who no longer need things, things you can sell. Maybe you've loaned money out to people starting small business and then they can't repay you."

She grinned. "Such things have happened," she said.

"I could use a partner who knows how to acquire things," he said. "I can sell them, but I need a picker."

"A picker?"

"Someone who finds good things for me to sell."

"I would be a good picker," she said. "And a better partner."

"Partner?"

"Someone who runs your operation in The Philippines and Hong Kong." She turned to him. "My sister works in Hong Kong, and she finds things, too. Sometimes very interesting old things."

"That might be good. It would be best if she'd work for you, though."

She took his arm. "We will settle this business at the bank, then you buy me lunch and we can talk about this business deal."

"Fine."

"Are you married?" she asked.

"No," he said.

"You need to meet my sister. She is a very pretty girl."

Finding the bezel, quite likely the original, had been a miracle. Finding Rowena held promise for his business. But he had to accept that life was definitely changing, and if Rowena had her way, dramatically.

He needed to sharpen his negotiating skills.

THE END

J. Lee Porter

 J. Lee Porter is a former IT specialist, programmer and data analyst for banking, security, and government agencies. He left the IT world behind on July 4th, 2016, declaring it his personal independence day to travel the world full time in search of inspiration for his writing.

nomadicgiant.com

Ed Teja

 Ed Teja is a lifelong writer and denizen of the margins of the world. A martial artist, former magazine editor, musician, and Caribbean boat bum, he writes stories about the people he meets and places he goes — stories that reach deep into the odd corners of the world that often disappear into the margins, and tell of the amazing, often strange, people that inhabit those places.

Find many more of his stories at

https://books2read.com/ap/RDOKrx/Ed-Teja